THE PURIM SUPERHERO

For Lily, Robie, Sarah, Claire, Esther, and Eve, and Ursula, Johnny, Helena, and Rachel, the next generation at the costume party. — E.K.

Todah Rabah to the wonderful people at Keshet for your recognition, and for all your courageous work. A big shout-out to the children and staff of the Jewish Day School of Metropolitan Seattle, who made me wish I had more Purim books to share. Oolicans and Kermit-arms for Arwen, Clara, Liz, Rachel, Rebecca, Shannon, Susan, Susanmarie, and Sofia, beta-readers and cheerers-on. Special thanks to Byron for the aliens; next time I'll try to get some monkeys in there, too. And thank you to Lise Kreps and Sarah Kushner. Because. — E.K.

For my Dad. He will always be my Superhero. — M.B.

With special thanks to Keshet which sponsored the contest that inspired this story. Keshet is a national organization that works for the full equality and inclusion of lesbian, gay, bisexual, and transgender Jews in Jewish life, www.keshetonline.org.

KAR-BEN Publishing
A division of Lerner Publishing Group, Inc.
241 First Avenue North
Minneapolis, MN 55401 U.S.A.
800-4KARBEN

Website address: www.karben.com

Library of Congress Cataloging-in-Publication Data

Kushner, Elisabeth.
     The Purim superhero / by Elisabeth Kushner ; illustrated by Mike Byrne.
          p.   cm.
     Summary: Nate wants to dress as an alien for Purim but his friend wants him to wear a superhero costume like the other boys, so Nate seeks guidance from his Daddy and Abba, who advise that being yourself makes you stronger.
     ISBN 978-0-7613-9061-9 (lib. bdg. : alk. paper)
     [1. Costume—Fiction. 2. Peer pressure—Fiction. 3. Purim—Fiction. 4. Jews—United States—Fiction.]
I. Byrne, Mike, 1979– ill. II. Title.
PZ7.K96428Pur 2013
[E]—dc23   2012009504

Manufactured in the United States of America
1 – DP – 12/31/12

THE PURIM SUPERHERO

By Elisabeth Kushner   Illustrated by Mike Byrne

KAR-BEN
PUBLISHING

"What are you going to be for Purim?" Max whispered to Nate during Hebrew school.

"I want to be an alien," Nate whispered back.

"All the boys in class are going to be superheroes," said Max.

"All the boys?" Nate asked.

"Yep," Max answered.

Nate picked up a green marker and drew antennae on his Mordechai mask.

Nate loved aliens. He loved to draw them. He loved to read about them. Sometimes at night he looked out the window and wished for aliens to come to the backyard and tell him about other planets.

That night at dinner the family talked about Purim costumes.

"Will you make me a rock star costume?" Miri asked Abba, one of her dads.

"Sure," said Abba. "How about you, Nate?"

Nate's mouth was full of chicken soup, so he couldn't answer right away.

"Nate wants to be a superhero," said Miri. "He said so in carpool."

"Really?" said Daddy.

"I was all ready to make you an alien costume," said Abba.

Nate scrunched up his face. "I don't know," he said.

"Better decide soon," said Abba. "I'll need time to sew."

All week Nate thought about his Purim costume, and how much he liked aliens. He thought about being the only boy who wouldn't be a superhero.

"I'll be a superhero, too," he told Max the next Sunday.

"Which one?" asked Max. "I'm going to be Batman, Ethan will be Superman, and Sam and Noah are deciding. You have to pick one, too."

"I have to pick?" said Nate.

"Yep," said Max.

That night Abba's scissors snip-snip-snipped, cutting out Miri's rock star outfit. "Did you choose your costume?" he asked Nate.

Nate shook his head. "Max said I need to pick a superhero."

"Is Max your boss?" Abba asked.

"All the boys are going to be superheroes," said Nate.

"You know," Abba said, "not all boys have to be the same thing."

Nate thought about how most kids had a mom and dad, not a Daddy and an Abba.

"Abba?" Nate asked. "Do you ever just want to be like everybody else?"

Abba looked at Nate. "You know the Purim story," Abba said. "Queen Esther saved the Jews because she didn't hide who she was. She told King Ahashuerus she was Jewish, and that her people were in danger.

"Sometimes showing who you really are makes you stronger, even if you're different from other people."

Nate didn't think being different would make him stronger. He thought it would make him lonely. But he would miss being an alien.

"Daddy?" Nate asked at bedtime. "How many superheroes are there?" Daddy was a teacher. He would know.

"Lots," said Daddy, "and people keep making up more."

"You can make them up?"

"Sure," said Daddy. "A hero is someone brave and strong, on the outside or on the inside."

"Like Queen Esther," said Nate.

"Exactly," said Daddy. "And a superhero is just a hero with special powers."

Nate switched off the light. His brain was buzzing with ideas.

"Last chance to make your Purim costume," said Abba the next day.

"It's a surprise," said Nate. "If I tell you what I need, can you sew it?"

"Absolutely," said Abba.

"Daddy?" said Nate. "If I need things for my costume, can you buy them for me?"

"Sure," said Daddy.

"Miri?" said Nate. "If I need words for my costume, can you write them down?"

"What words?" asked Miri.

Nate told her.

That evening Nate came downstairs holding a paper bag. "My costume's a surprise," he said. "I'll put it on when we get to synagogue."

When they arrived, Rabbi Joanie was getting ready to read the Megillah. Max was dressed like Batman and waving his grogger. The other boys from class had superhero costumes, too.

Nate went into the bathroom. He put on the alien suit Abba had sewed, and the antenna and mask Daddy had bought.

He taped on the big badge he had made with words Miri had written.

He unfolded a green towel and tied it around his neck for a cape.

When he was ready, Nate slipped into the costume parade.

"Time for prizes!" called Rabbi Joanie.

Miri won Most Glamorous. Max and Ethan and Sam and Noah all won Most Heroic.

Every kid had a prize, except Nate.
Had Rabbi Joanie forgotten him?

But then she waved to him to come up front. "And the award for Most Original goes to Nate! Please take a bow, and tell us about your costume."

"Well," said Nate, "like my badge says, I'm Super Alien. Super Alien has special powers that allow him to fly to Earth from another planet without a spaceship. He's brave and he's a hero."

"I've never seen a Super Alien before," said Rabbi Joanie. "That's very original."

Abba and Daddy and Miri clapped and smiled big smiles.

Afterward, at the carnival, Nate ran to the beanbag toss. Ethan was there too.

"I like your costume," said Ethan. "Aliens are cool. I should've been Super Puppy. I love puppies." He put a beanbag on his head. "Next Purim, let's be whatever we want."

"Maybe next Purim I'll be a Puppy Alien." Nate put a beanbag on his head, too. "And go beep-woof!" The beanbag fell off.

Ethan grinned. "Woof-beep!" he said.

And he and Nate both laughed.

About Purim

Purim, a holiday that comes in early spring, recalls how brave Queen Esther saved the Jewish people of Persia from wicked Haman's evil plot to destroy them. The story is recounted in the biblical Book of Esther. Families celebrate by wearing costumes, eating three-cornered cookies called hamentaschen, listening to the reading of the Megillah (a scroll containing the story) and making noise with groggers, blotting out the name of the villain Haman.

About the Author

Elisabeth Kushner lives in Vancouver, Canada, with her family and a jumble of books and musical instruments. If she were a superhero, she'd be Orange Ukulele Girl. Her favorite kind of hamentaschen is poppyseed. This is her first children's book.

About the Illustrator

Mike Byrne grew up near Liverpool in the United Kingdom, moving to London to work as an illustrator by day and a crayon wielding crime fighter by night. He lives in the English countryside with his wife and two cats, where he spends his days doodling and creating children's books.